# CHAPTER 1

# Space Truckers

The spaceship *Helios* shook hard and Max Nova missed the hand rail. He floated across the cargo bay and bounced off a crate.

"Whoa!" he shouted.

Darius, the ship's loader who was as strong as an ox, grabbed Max and pulled him to the rail. "You good, kid?" he asked.

The lights in the cargo bay flickered and a siren blasted out.

Max nodded. "Just a bit terrified. That's all."

Juno, the ship's engineer, floated past. She smacked the big fuse box on the wall of the bay with a spanner and the flickering stopped. "Company's cutting corners again," she grumbled. "This heap of junk's only held together by my hard work and sweat!"

Darius grinned. "Good thing we've got you, Juno. Or else we'd be space toast."

Another jolt shook the ship. Juno frowned. "Is the captain going to crash into *every* meteoroid in Space?"

Max's heart pounded. His father was the captain on the *Helios* and Max had joined him on this supply trip for an adventure … not a disaster!

Max pulled himself up the ladder into the cockpit. His father, Captain Sol Nova, sat in the command chair. He was calm and focused as he stared through the cockpit window at the vast darkness of Space. Vega, the ship's navigator,

# NOVA

# Also by Chris Bradford ...

## THE COSMOS SERIES

*Lunar*

*Stellar*

## THE VIRTUAL KOMBAT SERIES

*Gamer*

*Virus*

*Cyborg*

## THE NINJA SERIES

*First Mission*

*Death Touch*

*Assassin*

*S.P.E.A.R.*

For more information on Chris and his books visit:

**www.chrisbradford.co.uk**

# NOVA

## CHRIS BRADFORD

Illustrated by
### Charlotte Grange

Barrington Stoke

Published by Barrington Stoke
An imprint of HarperCollins*Publishers*
1 Robroyston Gate, Glasgow, G33 1JN

www.barringtonstoke.co.uk

HarperCollins*Publishers*
Macken House, 39/40 Mayor Street Upper,
Dublin 1, DO1 C9W8, Ireland

First published in 2026

Text © 2026 Chris Bradford
Illustrations © 2026 Charlotte Grange
Cover design © 2026 HarperCollins*Publishers* Limited

ISBN 978-0-00-870051-5

10 9 8 7 6 5 4 3 2 1

A catalogue record for this book is available from the British Library

Printed and bound in India by Replika Press Pvt. Ltd.

This book contains FSC™ certified paper and other controlled
sources to ensure responsible forest management.

For more information visit: www.harpercollins.co.uk/green

*To my Leo,*

*May the Light heal you*

# CONTENTS

was hunched over her console. She looked tense, her gaze fixed on the spinning rocks ahead.

"What's happening?" Max asked.

"We're passing through a debris trail from a comet. It leaves behind all these bits of dust and rock," his father told him.

"Brace yourself, rookie," said Vega as she gripped the controls. "It's about to get bumpy."

Max strapped himself into his seat just as a shower of rocks hit the ship. The *Helios* shuddered; red warning lights flashed.

"The shields are holding up," his father confirmed.

"For now," muttered Vega.

A meteoroid struck the hull and the whole ship rattled. Max gulped. "You said space travel was safe nowadays!"

"I did?" His father winked at him. "Welcome to space trucking, son."

# CHAPTER 2

## Anomaly

After a last big rumble, the ship stopped rocking and shaking. Everything went quiet. Vega let out a slow breath. "We're through."

Captain Sol nodded. "Nice navigating, Vega."

Max undid his seatbelt and floated to the cockpit window. Below, he could see the planet Mercury under the hot glare of the sun, which loomed three times larger than it did on Earth. The rocky surface of Mercury was rough and pitted with old craters – a grey, dead wasteland.

"Not exactly a holiday spot!" Max said.

"I never said it would be a holiday," replied his father. "Time to call home." He tapped his console. A moment later, Max's mother, Lyra, and his younger brother, Ziggy, popped up on the screen.

"Hey, Earthlings!" Sol greeted them. "Calling you as promised. We've reached Mercury."

Lyra smiled. "That's a relief."

Ziggy bounced up and down with excitement. "What's Mercury like, Dad?"

Max moved into the camera beside his father. "Small, dull and ugly – kind of like you, little bro!" he said with a grin.

Ziggy made a face. "Well, your head is like our solar system – full of empty space!"

"Stop it, you two!" their mother said. "How much space do you need *not* to bicker?"

"How about another galaxy?" Ziggy shot back.

Before Max could reply, their father cut in. "Mercury is the smallest and fastest planet in our solar system, Ziggy. It's the closest to the sun and has almost no atmosphere, so temperatures change from freezing cold at night to blazing hot in the day. Hot enough to melt lead!"

"Just like Darius's breath!" joked Juno as she floated into the cockpit with Darius next to her.

Darius grunted. "Careful, or I'll blow you out of the airlock."

Max tried not to laugh. Then the comms unit beeped, suddenly ending the call home.

"*Helios*, this is Star Haul Control. Change of plan," said a robotic voice. "You're being diverted."

Captain Sol frowned. "Diverted? But we're here to pick up iron ore."

"We've detected an anomaly near the sun," Control replied. "You need to investigate."

Max turned to Vega. "What's an anomaly?" he whispered.

"Something that's different from normal," she replied.

"And whatever ain't normal," Juno added, "often ain't good."

## CHAPTER 3

# Control

Moments later, a new destination flashed on the screen.

Captain Sol frowned. "That's dangerously close to the sun!"

Max's stomach twisted. Juno and Darius exchanged a worried look.

His father's face turned serious. "We're space truckers, not explorers. We're not trained for this."

"You only need to observe and report," Control replied.

Vega shook her head. "The *Helios* isn't built for close solar passes. The ship can't go that near to the sun."

"Can't we send a probe instead?" said Darius.

"Yeah," agreed Juno. "A probe doesn't have a live crew that'll cook inside it when it gets toasted by the sun!"

Control's voice crackled through the comms. "You're the closest spacecraft. You're still at speed and can slingshot off Mercury's gravity. Time is critical."

"Why the rush?" his father asked.

"There's a chance this anomaly is the start of a supernova."

Vega scoffed. "Impossible. The sun isn't big enough to go supernova and explode."

"Then what do you think it is?" asked Max.

"That's for you to find out," replied Control.

Darius crossed his big brawny arms. "Do we get a danger bonus?"

"You get overtime," Control replied.

Juno snorted. "That's *all*? Great!"

Captain Sol looked thoughtful. "And if we refuse?" he asked.

"Then you'll all have to find another job when you get back. This is a company order."

The call ended. Silence filled the cockpit.

Captain Sol turned to his crew. "Looks like we have no choice. We've got to do what they say," he said with a sigh.

Juno punched the wall in anger. "We're just tools for Star Haul, aren't we?"

"At least we get overtime," said Darius with a shrug.

Vega checked her calculations on the navigation console. "This will add over two weeks to our trip."

"That means I'll miss the start of school!" said Max, trying not to grin.

# CHAPTER 4

## Sunburn

As the *Helios* got closer and closer to the sun, Max stared in awe at its colossal size and raw power.

The sun's surface boiled and bubbled like a sea of fire. Flaming plasma exploded in huge arcs, and solar flares twisted in dazzling patterns.

Even the dark windows of the *Helios* cargo ship and their shields couldn't block the blazing light – or its scorching heat.

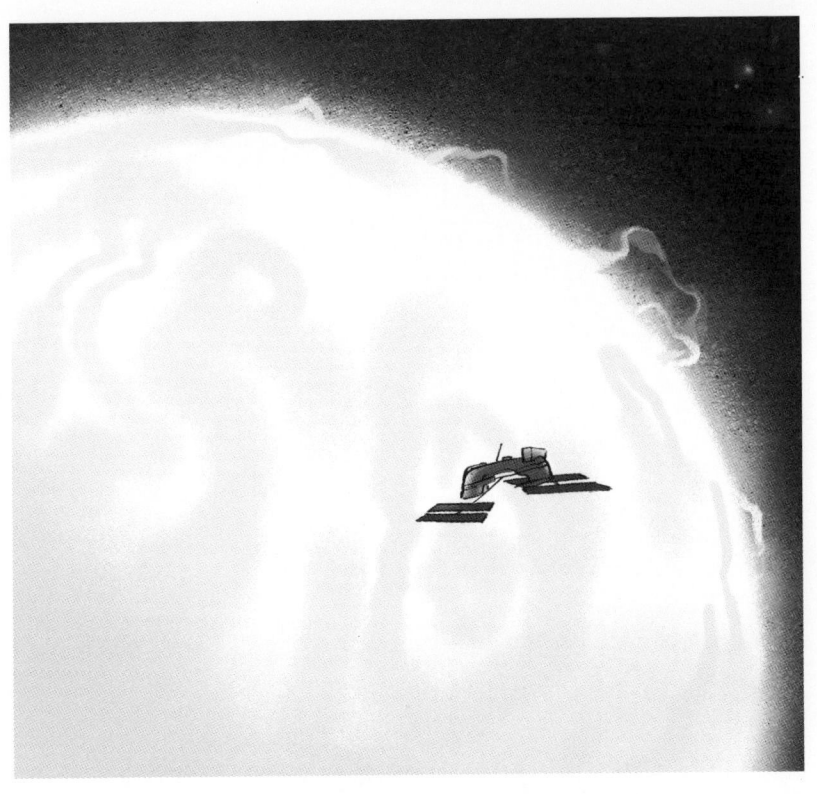

"Instant suntan, anyone?" Darius joked, slipping on a pair of sunglasses.

"More like instant sunburn," shot back Juno. "Without the heat shields, we'd be a dripping ball of molten metal in seconds."

Captain Sol wiped sweat from his forehead. A red warning light flashed on the console.

"The heat shields have reached their limit," he said. "We can't risk getting any nearer."

Vega nodded and adjusted the controls. The ship began to turn away from the sun.

Then the comms unit crackled to life.

"*Helios* ... this is ... Star Haul Control," the speaker said between bursts of static. "Have you ... spotted the ... anomaly?"

The crew peered out. The vacuum of Space lay ahead, empty and silent.

"There's nothing there," Captain Sol reported. "Your readings must be false."

"Readings are accurate," replied Control. "The *Helios* is closing in. Look again."

Max glanced up at the port hole in the cockpit ceiling.

And that's when he saw it ...

# CHAPTER 5

# Wormhole

The spaceship's sensors beeped loudly and lights blinked all across the cockpit's console.

"I'm picking up something *very* strange," Vega said as she peered at the readings on the console. "It's like ... Space itself is *bending*."

Max's mouth fell open as he stared at the anomaly. Floating above the *Helios* was a massive ball of swirling light. Inside, thousands of stars and galaxies spun round and round just like a snow globe that's been shaken.

"What is *that*?" Max asked.

Vega looked up and gasped. "That's a wormhole!"

"A what?" Max blinked.

His father got up and floated next to Max. He grinned at the wondrous sight. "A wormhole is a shortcut through Space," he explained. "Space is *huge* – so huge that even the fastest ships would take thousands of years to reach the nearest stars. But a wormhole bends Space and shortens the journey."

Max frowned. "How can that happen? Does Space really *bend*?"

His father tore a sheet of paper from his logbook and held it up. "Imagine this paper is Space. Normally, if you wanted to get from one edge to the other, you'd have to cross the whole page."

He took out a pencil and drew two circles at opposite edges of the paper, then he drew a long line from one circle to the other. "Now watch this."

He folded the paper in half so that the two circles touched.

"This is what happens in a wormhole. It bends Space like folding paper. Then you just go through the wormhole" – he jabbed the pencil through the folded paper – "and *boom*! Instant galactic shortcut."

"Wow!" said Max. His brain reeled. "That's mind- as well as Space-bending!"

"This will be the first wormhole anyone's actually seen though," said Vega. "Up to now, wormholes were just a theory."

"So where does the wormhole go?" Darius asked.

"Who knows?" Juno muttered. "To be honest, I'm not that keen to find out."

"Agreed," said Captain Sol. "Vega, move us to a safe distance."

Before Vega could change course, the comms crackled into life with a burst of static. "*Helios* ... proceed closer ... full data sweep required."

"Too dangerous, Control," replied Sol. "We're a cargo ship, not an exploration vessel."

"Captain, this is an order," came the cold reply.

Max saw his father clench his fist. He didn't appear to want to follow the order. They all knew that going any closer was risky. But so was disobeying orders. Captain Sol chewed his lip as he thought hard about his decision.

"Then I refuse," he said at last.

"Understood," Control replied.

The *Helios* suddenly veered towards the wormhole.

Captain Sol turned to Vega. "What are you doing?" he snapped.

Vega jabbed at the controls. "It's not me!" she shouted. "The ship's on automatic pilot – I'm locked out!"

"Control!" Sol barked. "Return command of my ship – now!"

"The *Helios* is the property of Star Haul," Control said matter-of-factly.

Max grabbed his father's hand. He felt very scared. Their ship was headed closer to the sun – and straight towards the swirling mouth of the wormhole!

# CHAPTER 6

## Burnout

The cockpit was getting hotter and hotter. Sweat dripped down Max's face as alarms blared and radiation warnings flashed red across the control screens. The *Helios* groaned and creaked like an old ship in a storm.

Darius wiped his forehead. "Is it just me or are we roasting like chickens in here?"

"More like flame-grilled," Juno muttered as sparks burst from a control panel. The smell of burning electronics filled the air.

Captain Sol gripped his chair, his voice tight. "Control, respond! Redirect *Helios* now!" Static hissed through the speakers. "Control, do you read?"

"We've lost radio contact," Vega said as she stabbed at the buttons on her console. "Too much solar radiation."

"Or Control's just ignoring us," Juno said.

Captain Sol slammed his fist angrily on the console. "Go to manual! Juno, Darius – sever the remote link!"

"We're on it!" Darius yelled. He and Juno pushed off, floating towards the server room.

"Are we going to … *die*?" Max asked.

His father shook his head. "No, son. I've been in worse spots than this before."

Max stared at him in disbelief. "Worse than flying towards a wormhole, next to the sun, in a melting tin can?"

His father replied with a tight-lipped smile. "Well ... maybe not *this* bad."

Suddenly, the ship's systems flickered and died. The steady hum of the engines vanished. The cockpit fell silent. Then ...

*CRACKLE!* Sparks rained down as every display went dark.

Max's stomach dropped. "Uh ... did they just cut the power?"

Captain Sol shouted down to the server room. "I didn't tell you to shut everything down!" he barked to Juno and Darius.

"We didn't," Juno shouted back. "The whole system fried itself."

# CHAPTER 7

# Life-Craft

Heat surged through the ship. Without the engines running, the shields stopped working. The *Helios* was caught in the sun's gravity and slowly spiralling towards destruction.

Juno and Darius raced to reboot the systems. Max could hear the clang of her spanner.

At last, the emergency power kicked in. Captain Sol called down, "Juno, can we restart the engines?"

"No," Juno replied. "They need to cool down. And guess what? They can't do that this close to the sun."

"Then we have to evacuate," said Sol.

Max gasped. "Evacuate? Where to?"

"We need to get to the life-crafts!" Sol said, and leapt from his seat. "Move!"

They headed out of the cockpit and down towards the life-crafts in the loading bay. Max felt his blood pounding in his ears as he tried to keep up. The heat pressed around him like a heavy blanket. It became hard to breathe.

Juno reached the first life-craft and yanked the lever to open the hatch. But it didn't move. She pulled again. "No! The hatch is jammed! It must be the heat."

Darius tried the second life-craft. "This one's down too!"

They checked the others.  Only one hatch was working.

Juno turned to Sol with a grim look.  "The life-craft is only big enough for one person."

Captain Sol looked at his crew, who all nodded.

Max knew what was coming and he felt terrible about it.  He shook his head.

"You're going," his father insisted.  "No arguments."

"I'm not leaving you!" said Max.

Sol pushed Max towards the open hatch. "We'll try to restart the ship.  But you have to survive."

Max began to cry.  "Dad ... no ... we'll find another way ... together."

"There is no other way," his father said. He pulled Max into a hug. "You need to go, Max. Now."

"I don't want to leave you," Max croaked.

"Go, Max!" his father commanded. "That's an order."

Vega fitted Max with a helmet and Darius clapped him on the back. "Guess I get to blow *you* out the airlock, kid."

Max didn't laugh at Darius's joke. He just wanted to cry.

"Go! Before it's too late!" insisted Juno. She pulled the lever and the hatch hissed open.

Max climbed inside the life-craft, his hands shaking. The door shut behind him and he strapped himself into the seat. He saw his father through the small window. His eyes

were red with tears. His father mouthed a
silent *I love you*. Then the life-craft launched.

Max watched as his life-craft sped away
from the *Helios*, while the cargo ship drifted
ever closer to the sun.

"No …" Max sobbed.  He pressed his gloved hand to the window and waved sadly.  He'd lost them – his father, Juno, Darius, Vega – all of them.

Suddenly, his life-craft lurched to the side. The straps of the harness dug into Max as he was thrown around.  All he could see from the life-craft's window was a whirling vortex of impossible colours.  Max screamed as he was sucked into the wormhole.

# CHAPTER 8

# Through the Wormhole

Max's life-craft shot through Space at terrifying speed. The force pinned him against his seat. He gritted his teeth and his stomach flipped. He felt like he was on the world's worst rollercoaster. The life-craft rattled and groaned, on the point of tearing apart.

"Please hold together," Max begged.

Outside the window, colours streaked past – reds, blues and dazzling yellows. Stars twisted and stretched, then snapped back into swirling shapes, making Max's head spin. Time itself seemed to warp – speeding up and slowing down all at once. His body tingled. It felt strangely light and super heavy at the same time. He struggled to breathe and his heart raced.

Just when Max thought he and the life-craft couldn't take any more, everything stopped.

No sound. No movement. Just stillness.

Max gasped for breath. His fingers trembled as he gripped the edge of the small control panel. "I'm alive," he croaked. "I made it through the wormhole!"

He turned to the window. "But where am I?"

Stars shone all around, but not in any pattern he knew. Instead of a sun, there was a supermassive black hole in the centre of this new space system. A glowing ring of light spun around its dark core, pulsing like a heartbeat.

"I'm in another galaxy!" Max murmured.

Then things got even stranger. Ahead of Max was a planet unlike anything he'd ever even dreamed of. It gleamed like a giant crystal and the surface rippled with a rainbow of colours under the weird starlight.

And his life-craft was rocketing straight for it.

Max's heart thudded harder. "No, no, no!" He pressed every button on the console. Nothing worked. He was out of control and falling fast.

As the life-craft dived down through the planet's atmosphere, the nose cone glowed red. The cabin shook and became hotter and hotter.

"Slow down!" Max yelled as he punched at more buttons. Still the life-craft didn't respond.

The ground rushed towards him – an endless glass-like span of glittering crystal.

At the last second, the life-craft's emergency thrusters fired into action. The life-craft skidded and bounced as it landed, sending up clouds of sparkling dust. Max gripped on to his seat. Then …

*CRASH!*

The life-craft slammed into a towering wall of crystal. His helmet smacked against the window and everything went black.

# CHAPTER 9

# Strange New World

Max groaned. A shrill alarm bleeped inside the cabin. The noise made his head hurt even more. Every part of his body was bruised and he tasted blood in his mouth where he'd bitten his tongue. Slowly, he opened his eyes.

Through the cracked window, he saw a strange new world. A landscape of glittering crystal reflected the odd glow from the black hole in the sky.

Max unstrapped himself. He hurt all over and it was hard to move. He forced open the life-craft's hatch and clambered out. His boots crunched on the glassy ground, which rippled with colours under his feet.

*I survived*, he thought, dazed. *But now what?*

He looked slowly around at the alien planet. The sky above swirled purple and gold. The black hole – with its glowing ring of light – stared down at him like some giant eye.

Max took a step forwards and nearly fell over. The gravity here was much stronger than on Earth. Every movement felt slow, like he was wading through thick water. He checked his smartwatch. The clock showed less than an hour had passed since he'd left the *Helios*.

The *Helios*! *His father!*

Max began to panic.  He climbed back into the life-craft and flipped on the comms unit. "Dad? *Helios*, do you read me?" he shouted.

Silence.

He tried again.  Nothing – not even static.

Max clenched his fists and tried to stay calm.  He scanned the horizon of the new planet.  Maybe there was life here.  Maybe someone – or something – could help him get back to Planet Earth.  Whatever, he couldn't just sit here and wait for rescue.  No one was coming.  Not in this distant galaxy.  He had to find a way to survive and get home.

Max got out of the life-craft and began to climb a jagged hill of crystal so that he could see where he was.  Each step sent ripples of rainbow-coloured lights through the rocks. At the top of the hill, he stopped for a rest.

Everywhere he looked, there were tall towers made of crystal. They looked like huge cities. But they stood still and silent. Max could see no sign of life at all.

A wave of despair hit him. As he turned back towards the life-craft, his boot slipped on the smooth crystal. He slid down the slope on his back.

As he fell, he crashed into a spike of rock. Pain shot through his hand as a sharp crystal cut through his glove. A cold electric shock zapped through his fingers. Max rolled to the bottom of the hill, landing hard.

His helmet hit the ground with a crack and he heard a soft hiss as air began to leak from his visor.

# CHAPTER 10

## Cocoon

Max lay crumpled on the ground. His hand stung where the crystal had cut through his glove and into his skin. An alarm sounded in his helmet, a red warning light blinking on his safety display – his oxygen levels were dropping fast!

"No!" gasped Max. *He couldn't breathe!*

He didn't want to die here. Not alone. Not so far from home.

Everything turned dark as precious oxygen leaked out. The alarm faded into the distance.

Max's body grew heavy. His eyes began to close. He couldn't stay awake.

Then something incredible happened.

The crystal that had cut into him began to glow – a soft green light pulsed in the palm of his hand through his glove. Max blinked. Was he imagining it? Then the ground shifted. Crystal spikes sprouted around him. They curled and twisted like glass vines. They stretched towards Max and wrapped around his hand.

Max gasped in horror as the glowing crystal vines crept up his arm. He tried to pull himself free but the vines were as strong as steel. They coated his arm and began to creep across his chest.

"NO, STOP!" Max shouted. "Leave me alone!"

He thrashed around. The crystal pulsed purple and suddenly Max felt calm. His muscles

went slack and he didn't feel scared any longer. He watched with interest as the crystal vines wrapped his body in a purple cocoon.

The crystal flowed over his helmet and filled the crack in his visor. Max's chest felt tight. He gasped for air as the last of his oxygen ran out!

The world around him blurred.  A rainbow of colours swirled before his eyes and he fell into a trance.  Slowly, the colours turned into sounds, then into shapes.  Weird alien faces flickered around him – shimmering beings made of crystal and light.

Somehow Max knew he wasn't alone ...

# CHAPTER 11

# The Luminites

Max opened his eyes wide.  Was he alive?  Was he dreaming?

He was no longer wrapped in the crystal cocoon.  The crack in his visor had gone, filled with a smooth glass-like layer.  He was breathing normally.  His oxygen levels were stable.

Slowly, Max sat up and flexed his fingers.  His hand, where the crystal had cut through his glove, was healed and the hole in his glove had been fixed too.  But he could still *feel* something – a tiny shard deep in his palm still glowed.  It felt cold yet oddly warm at the same time.

"What happened to me?" Max rasped.

*We saved you*, someone replied softly.

Max spun around in shock.  "Who said that?" he asked.

The crystal rocks pulsed with colour, and the voice echoed in his mind.  *Speaking is slow and primitive.  Thoughts are quicker – although still slower than light.*

Max froze.  "What do you mean?" he said out loud.

The colours got brighter.  *Think, and we will hear you.*

Max's fear faded.  He was now more puzzled than scared.  *Where are you?* he thought carefully.  *Show yourself.*

The colours around him formed into flickering shapes. Max saw beings made of pure light floating inside the crystals.

*What are you?* Max asked in his thoughts.

The crystals pulsed again. *In your language, you might call us ... Luminites.*

Max frowned. *But how can I hear you in my head?*

*The crystal in your hand connects us*, the voice replied. *It acts as a bridge between our minds.*

Max looked down at the dot of light glowing through his glove. *But you're aliens. How come I understand you?*

The Luminites shone with warmth. *To us, you are the alien. But we have looked into your mind and learned how your kind work. That's why we can communicate with you and heal your body.*

Max closed his hand. *Thank you*, he thought. *What's your name? Who am I speaking to?*

*All of us*, the voice replied. *We are one yet many.*

Max's mind throbbed. He didn't understand and it hurt to think so hard. *What do you want with me?* His thoughts flashed to every scary movie he'd seen about aliens.

Laughter echoed in his head. *No, we don't want to dissect you or eat you, Max! We want to help.*

*How?* Max asked.

An electric blue line snaked across the ground, glowing as it wound up and over the hill.

*Follow the path*, instructed the Luminites, *and you will find out.*

## CHAPTER 12

# Library of Time

In a daze, Max followed the path of blue light. It led him up the slope, over the hill and into a city made of crystal. Now that he was closer, he saw he'd been wrong when he thought the crystal towers were dead. The city was full of life. The Luminites flickered within the glassy rocks, their bright forms shifting and glowing like living stars.

He walked along the path to a huge crystal tower. It gleamed like a giant jewel under the swirling purple and gold sky.

*What is this place?* he asked.

The calm voice of the Luminites answered, *We call this the Library of Time.*

Max gasped as he stepped inside. He had to shield his eyes. The interior was dazzling – it was like stepping into a kaleidoscope. Every surface reflected thousands of tiny spinning galaxies.

At the centre of the huge chamber, a Luminite floated inside a tall crystal pyramid. *We are Watchers of the Universe*, it explained. *And this is where we've stored all our knowledge – it's the Library of Time and Space, where past, present and future exist together in the fifth dimension.*

Max gave the Luminite a puzzled look. *I know the first three dimensions – length, width, and height – like the sides of a cube. The fourth dimension is ... time, I think. But what's the fifth dimension?*

*You are correct! The fourth dimension is time*, said the Luminite, radiating what felt like warmth. *For your kind, time moves in one direction only – forwards. But as beings of light, we see all time all at once. That is the fifth dimension.*

Max frowned. *I don't get it.*

*Picture time as pages in a book*, the Luminite explained. *Your kind can read one page at a time, in one direction, forwards. But we can read any page, in any order, backwards or forwards, or even flip through the entire book at once.*

Max thought for a moment, a spark of understanding forming. *So ... is my galaxy in your Library of Time?*

*Of course!*

A nearby crystal burst into light. A swirling galaxy shone inside it. Max watched as the view zoomed in, past distant stars, until he was looking at his own solar system.  The zoom got closer and closer to the sun.

Then Max saw it.

The *Helios*.

The spaceship was spinning towards the blazing sun, its hull glowing red-hot as it burned up in the intense heat.

"Dad!" Max shouted.  His heart pounded. His throat felt tight.  Tears stung his eyes.

*Do not worry*, the Luminite told him. *You can save your father and the crew.*

"But how?" he asked.  "It's too late."

The Luminite's glow pulsed gently.  *There is no such thing as too late in the fifth dimension. You have all the time in the universe.*

# CHAPTER 13

# Gravity Wave

Max stared at the *Helios* as it darted towards the sun. He grasped the crystal in his hands. *How can I save the* Helios? he screamed inside.

*Gravity is the only force that crosses Space and time,* the Luminite explained. *You can use a gravity wave to push your father's spaceship to safety.*

Max blinked. *Me?*

*Yes,* replied the Luminite. *You've been touched by our Light. We've learned from you,*

*and now you will learn from us. Place your*
*hand on the pyramid where you can see me.*

Max took a deep breath, then slowly pressed
his hand to the cool edge of the pyramid where
the Luminite floated. The moment his glove
made contact, energy surged through his body.
His hand glowed brightly and his heart pounded
as waves of new alien learning filled his mind.

Max felt his brain heating up. But when at last he pulled his hand away, he knew what he had to do.

Max shook from the energy in his body. *Why are you helping me?* he asked.

*We may be alien to one another, but love is universal*, the Luminite replied. *Use that love to save your father.*

Max turned to the crystal that showed him his solar system and the *Helios*. He put his hand on the ship and thought of his father, Vega, Juno and Darius. He felt a rush of love for them, a force so strong that it could cross galaxies.

"Time to turn towards home, Dad," he whispered.

Max pictured a powerful gravity wave that could push the ship away from danger. The crystal pulsed under his hand. His thoughts became stronger and stronger. The view in the crystal's surface shifted – the *Helios* shuddered, then veered sharply away from the sun's deadly pull.

Max gave a sigh of relief as he watched the spaceship escape the inferno and head back towards open Space.

The *Helios* and its crew were safe.

## CHAPTER 14

# The Hole Home

Max stood outside the Library of Time, looking up at the alien sky. It was night, and the swirling purple and gold clouds had turned into a velvety black. The giant, unblinking eye of the black hole loomed above him. But Max was not focused on the black hole.

Instead of stars, the sky was filled with wormholes, too many to count. They gleamed like round spinning windows. Were they shortcuts to other worlds?

Max sighed. He felt both relief and sadness. His father and the crew were safe now and heading back towards Earth. But Max was still stuck on the alien planet.

"Which hole takes me home?" he said out loud.

*You're welcome to stay*, the Luminites replied. *But if you wish to return, this is the portal to choose.*

One of the wormholes in the sky became especially bright. It pulsed with warm and inviting colours.

Max frowned. *But how can I get there? I don't have a spacecraft*, he thought.

*That problem is easy to fix*, the Luminites told him. *But be aware that time has passed for you at home.*

Max glanced at his smartwatch. Less than a day had gone by since he left the *Helios*.

*I won't be far behind them*, he thought. *They've only just turned for home and I haven't been on this planet for long.*

*Time works differently here because of the black hole*, the Luminites explained.

*What do you mean?* Max asked.

*Gravity affects time*, the Luminites went on. *The stronger gravity is, the slower time moves. Gravity works like stepping on the brakes of a car. The black hole in our system has very strong gravity. So for every day on our planet, years can pass on Earth.*

*Oh no!* thought Max in panic. *Then I don't have a second to lose. I need to get home now!*

## CHAPTER 15

# Crystal Ship

*Max, return to your ship*, the Luminites commanded.

*But it's destroyed*, Max thought.

He heard what sounded like a chuckle of laughter. *Not any more.*

Max dashed along the electric blue path back to his craft. Every step was difficult in the planet's strong gravity, but his body was full of fresh energy.

At the top of the hill, he stopped and stared in amazement. His life-craft – or what had once been his life-craft – now formed the cockpit of a huge crystal starship. The sleek spacecraft shone like an arrow of glass.

Max bounded down the slope as quickly as the planet's heavy gravity would let him. He stepped up to the starship and ran his hand along its smooth, cool hull. It shimmered with shifting colours. He couldn't believe what he was looking at.

*We've built you a new starship*, said the Luminites. *We've blended our technology with yours. This ship can travel between galaxies and reach light speed. We hope you like it.*

"Like it? I LOVE it!" Max shouted, his voice echoing off the crystal rocks and towers. "Thank you!"

Max climbed a crystal gangway and entered the cockpit. The interior was like nothing he'd ever seen – there were smooth glass surfaces and beams of light instead of control switches and levers. They glowed under his touch.

*How do I fly it?* Max asked as he got into the pilot's seat.

*Simply place your hand on the console and think of where you want to go*, the Luminites explained. *The entire ship is controlled by thought alone.*

Max didn't wait another second. He placed his hand on the console. Instantly, the ship's controls lit up, its engines humming into life.

*Wow!* thought Max. *This is incredible. How can I ever thank you?*

*Use the knowledge and starship we've given you to explore Space and learn about your place in the universe*, the Luminites replied.

*Will we ever meet again?* Max asked.

His gloved hand glowed softly in reply.

*You will always be part of us, Max*, said the Luminites. *A splinter of our light now lives within you.*

# CHAPTER 16

# Light Speed

Max took a deep breath and thought of home. The crystal starship lifted off the ground. As the starship soared into the sky, the towers of the Crystal City flickered with multicoloured light as though the Luminites were waving goodbye.

With a last look back, Max held up his glowing hand and waved. Then he shot off into the night. He watched through the cockpit window as the purple and gold sky melted away.

The ship glided smoothly through Space, accelerating to an incredible speed. Stars and wormholes stretched and warped around him

like streaks of liquid light.  The black hole in the distance seemed to contract, almost as if it were blinking.

Max held on tightly to his seat as the ship dived into the swirling vortex of the wormhole. But this time, the crystal starship remained steady.  As it cruised through the wormhole, its Light Engines hummed.  The ship's systems – pulsing with alien technology – felt like they were a part of Max himself.  His thoughts controlling the ship.

Stars and planets flew past.  Time seemed to stretch and squash, twirling in a dance of Space and light.

Then, with a sudden jolt, Max burst from the wormhole.  The spiralling chaos vanished and the stillness of Space returned.

A brilliant sun blazed before him.  But his starship stayed cool – its crystal hull reflected back the intense heat and solar radiation.

Max scanned the stars and soon spotted patterns he knew. In the distance, he spied a small, grey, dull planet – Mercury.

He was home! Back in his own solar system!

But he couldn't see the *Helios* anywhere. His scanners picked up nothing either. Suddenly, Max's excitement turned to worry.

Then he remembered. The Luminites had told him – time moved differently on their planet. The *Helios* must be further along in its journey.

With a single thought, Max commanded the ship to head for Earth. The Light Engines thrummed and Max was pressed back into his seat. The starship zipped past Mercury at startling speed, then shot by Venus.

Moments later, the blue-green orb of Earth came into view. Max's heart burst with joy and amazement. Rather than weeks, he was home in minutes!

# CHAPTER 17

# Five Years

Max didn't need to tell the starship where to land on Earth – it already knew. The only problem was finding a good landing site. In the end, it touched down in an old parking lot next to his block of flats.

As the Light Engines powered down, Max spotted people peering out of their windows. Some looked scared, others excited. A crowd soon came together in the parking lot and stood around the gleaming starship.

Max unstrapped himself and stepped down from the cockpit onto the cracked tarmac.

He waved to the crowd.

"Hey, Earthlings!" he called out as a joke, remembering his father's greeting aboard the *Helios*.

The crowd shifted nervously.

"It's an alien invasion!" someone gasped.

People began to back away.  Others picked up metal bars and bricks for weapons.

"No, I'm not an alien!" shouted Max.  He quickly took off his helmet.

Everyone went still.

"Max?" said a man's voice.

The crowd parted as two people walked slowly up to the starship.  Max knew them – they were his parents!  But they were different.  His father looked older and sadder, his hair now flecked with grey.  His mother's face was lined with wrinkles and her eyes glistened with tears.

"Max, is that really you?" his father croaked.

Max nodded.  "Hi, Dad.  I'm home."

His mother pressed a hand to her mouth.  "Max, you've been missing for five years!"

Max staggered back a step.  "*Five years?*  But I only left the *Helios* in the life-craft yesterday!"  He held up his smartwatch to show them.

Then another person stepped from the crowd.  It was his brother, Ziggy.  He was tall and broad and looked the same age as Max.  He was no longer the little brother Max had left behind.

"Where have you been, bro?" Ziggy asked.

Max rubbed the back of his neck. "In another galaxy."

Ziggy snorted. "You're kidding, right? I was joking when I said you should go to another galaxy!"

Max grinned. "Well, it's not my fault that I got pulled into a wormhole. Then an alien species called the Luminites rescued me and now I'm back."

Ziggy prodded a finger into Max's chest. "How do we know it's *really* you? You could be an alien! You look exactly the same as you did five years ago."

"That's because of gravity and how it affects time," Max explained. He turned to his father. "Gravity also saved the *Helios*. Dad, I pushed your ship away from the sun with a gravity wave."

"What?" said Max's father. His mouth opened in shock. "So that explains why the *Helios* suddenly changed direction without any power all those years ago!"

Max nodded. "That was me."

His father pulled Max into a tight hug. "I thought I'd lost everything that day," he sobbed.

"I lost command of my ship ... my job ... almost my life ... but, worst of all, I thought I lost you."

"Don't worry, Dad," Max said with a big smile. "Our problems are over. You now have command of a new ship with advanced light technology. We can start our own company – NOVA Inter-Galactic Enterprises."

Max gestured towards the gleaming crystal starship. His gloved hand pulsed with light. "Our future is brighter than any star!"

Our books are tested
for children and young people by
children and young people.

Thanks to everyone who consulted on
a manuscript for their time and effort in
helping us to make our books better
for our readers.